Cheat Challenge

Cheat Challenge

Robin and Chris Lawrie

Illustrated by
Robin Lawrie

Acknowledgements

The authors and publishers would like to thank
Julia Francis, Hereford Diocesan Deaf Church
lay co-chaplain, for her help with the sign language
in the *Chain Gang* bo

Published by Evans Bro
2A Portman Mansions
Chiltern Street
London W1U 6NR

© Robin and Christine

First published 2001

WORCESTERSHIRE COUNTY COUNCIL	
128	
Cypher	08.02.02
	£3.99

Printed in Hong Kong

British Library Cataloguing in Publication data.
Lawrie, Robin
 Cheat Challenge. – (The Chain Gang)
 1. Slam Duncan (Fictitious character) – Juvenile fiction
 2. All terrain cycling – Juvenile fiction 3. Adventure stories
 4. Children's stories
 I. Title II. Lawrie, Chris
 823.9'14[J]

ISBN 0 237 52259 4

5

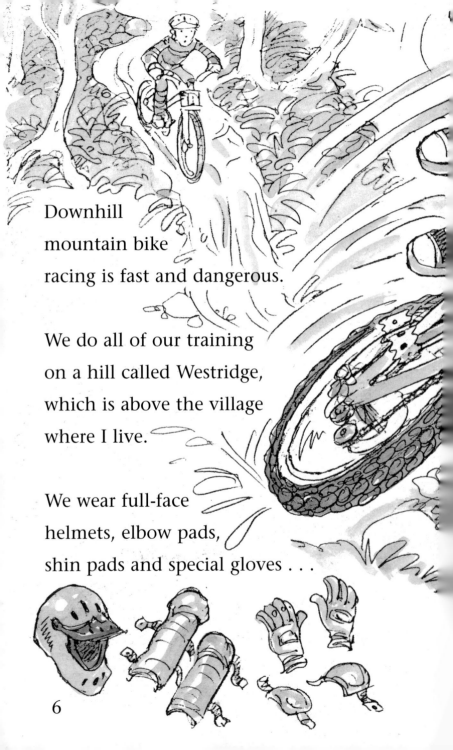

Downhill
mountain bike
racing is fast and dangerous.

We do all of our training
on a hill called Westridge,
which is above the village
where I live.

We wear full-face
helmets, elbow pads,
shin pads and special gloves . . .

6

. . . just in case
we fall off!

Oooh!

We race
against the clock.
The fastest time down
a course is the winner.
The courses are about a mile long.

7

Although Westridge looks like a forest, it's really a big tree farm. Some of the trees are harvested every ten years or so, and new ones are planted in their place.

Big machines are
used to cut and stack
the trees. If you are smart,
you stay well away . . .

* Amazing!

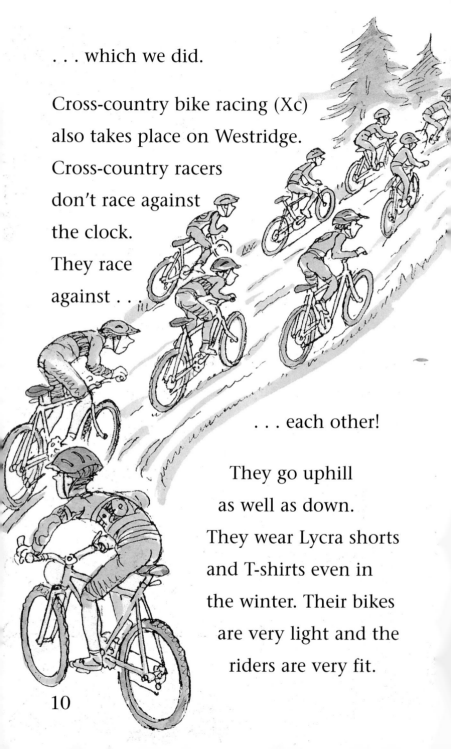

. . . which we did.

Cross-country bike racing (Xc) also takes place on Westridge. Cross-country racers don't race against the clock. They race against . . .

. . . each other!

They go uphill as well as down. They wear Lycra shorts and T-shirts even in the winter. Their bikes are very light and the riders are very fit.

They have to be
because the courses can
be six miles long and they
sometimes go round two or three times!

One day, Larry and I were training on
the cross-country side of Westridge,
well away from the tree fellers.
We overheard some cross-country
racers talking.

Yeah! Excalibur's well 'ard!

Yeah, I've heard it's pretty tough!

So, how come it's only for juveniles then?

So, what's Excalibur then?

It was a sword that belonged to King Arthur. He became King after he pulled it out of a stone when he was a boy.

Lots of people tried but only Arthur managed it, 'cos he was honest and good.

Hooray!

Hooray!

Arthur was a brilliant king. He had a round table where he and his knights talked things over. Because it was round, nobody was at the head of the table, so everybody had an equal say.

Chivalry, which means being fair and kind to everyone, even your enemies, was important to Arthur and his knights.

Spare me 'cos I am disarmed!

Oh, all right then.

When they weren't having battles, Arthur and his knights would have jousts, which were like pretend battles. The idea was to knock the other bloke off his horse and, if he was uninjured, you could then have a sword fight.

They, too, had full-face helmets and body armour but made of steel, not plastic.

Then, on the way home . . .

. . . Larry went too deep
into a corner.

He went crashing through the
undergrowth and hit something
very solid.

BANG

We pulled away the bracken
to see what it was. And were
amazed to find . . .

EXCALIBUR!

A wooden one!

This must have been
what those cross-country
lads were talking about.

But what does it mean?

Larry, of course, just had to have a go at pulling it out.

Nothing – not an inch.

Then me.

No future kings there then!

But when we got to Larry's place, we had some post.

NATIONAL CYCLING FEDERATION PRESENTS

Sword in the Stump
CHALLENGE

MOUNTAIN BIKE RACES

To promote fair play and understanding between cyclists

✓ 2 CROSS-COUNTRY RACES
✓ 2 DOWNHILL RACES
✓ 2 DUEL DESCENDERS

FEATURING!
eXcalibur
the new Xc course.
It's **wicked**

Later that week I was helping out in my dad's garage.

* Bob Turner – ace pro mountain biker and course designer.

While I was hoovering,

what should I see on the back seat . . .

Punk Tuer is a good biker but also a terrible cheat. His dad would certainly tell him where the new course was.

Hey, Punk, guess what!

Sure enough, next weekend Punk and his chum, "Dyno" Sawyer, were practising the right course.

Fionn, Larry, Dozy and Andy were sure the new course followed the old 1990 course because "90" is XC in Roman numbers.

What should I do? Should I tell them?

The trouble was,
the old "90" went right
through the tree-felling area.

I was in a terrible state.

24

Then it happened.

BANG!

Larry rode straight
into a log lifter.

*Oh no, oh no, oh no!
The poor boy has*
PASSED ON!

I was sure he was dead!
The driver was sure
he was dead!

So when he suddenly sat up,
the driver passed out.

THUD

But that wasn't all. While we were
trying to wake up the driver . . .

. . . the tractor
started to roll towards some walkers!

What the . . .!

Suddenly, Andy burst into the clearing and leapt into the cab.

I could see him madly pulling all the levers, looking for the handbrake.

ANDY!

Mutter mutter yak yak.

I was signing and yelling at him **"It's on the floor!"** but he didn't see and couldn't hear. The walkers were busy yakking and didn't hear me either.

Then things got really messy.

They just didn't understand.

The walkers apologised and made a fuss
of Andy. My nerves were in bits
and I just rode away . . .

* Wrong! Wrong!

. . . till I found the sword in the stump
near the end of the new course.

OK, Excalibur, what would Arthur do now? I've tried not to cheat and four people almost got killed. Punk Tuer is cheating and is getting mega practice on the new course. It's not fair.

Then I heard someone laughing.
Bob Turner and his mates were putting
up the course-marking tapes.
The big secret was out.
I didn't
have to worry
any more.

They'll need super glued saddles to stay on here!

HAW HAW

Soon, everybody was practising the new course.